Trouble on the Tracks

Kathy Mallat

Walker & Company

New York

For Meg, the true engineer behind this book

First published in the United States of America in 2001 by Walker Publishing Company, Inc.
Published simultaneously in Canada by Fitzhenry and Whiteside, Markham, Ontario L3R 4T8

Library of Congress Cataloging-in-Publication Data

Mallat, Kathy.
Trouble on the tracks / Kathy Mallat.
p. cm.
Summary: There's Trouble with a capital "T" lurking among the familiar faces as a train
makes its way through the villages along its route.
ISBN 0-8027-8771-1 — ISBN 0-8027-8773-8
[1. Railroads—Trains—Fiction. 2. Railroads—Models—Fiction. 3. Cats—Fiction.] I. Title.
PZ7.M29455 Tr 2001
[E]—dc21   00-054424

The illustrations were made on 24-ply Crescent illustration board using
Prismacolor permanent markers as a base and overlayed with Prismacolor colored pencils.

Book design by Bruce McMillan

Printed in Hong Kong
10 9 8 7 6 5 4 3 2 1

E
MAL

"All aboard! Next stop, Black Paw Crossing!"

Some last-minute passengers scurry on board.

The engineer makes his final check. "I hope
we don't run into trouble today."

The conductor gives the all-clear signal.
WOO-A-WOO blasts the whistle.

The train pulls away from the station,
gathering speed at a slow but steady pace.

Soon it's gliding along the tracks. It has
traveled this route many times before.

The engineer keeps a firm hand on the controls, as the train rolls through forests and farmland.

It rumbles through villages where faces are familiar.

It speeds along under the watchful eye of the
engineer . . . until he spots trouble ahead.

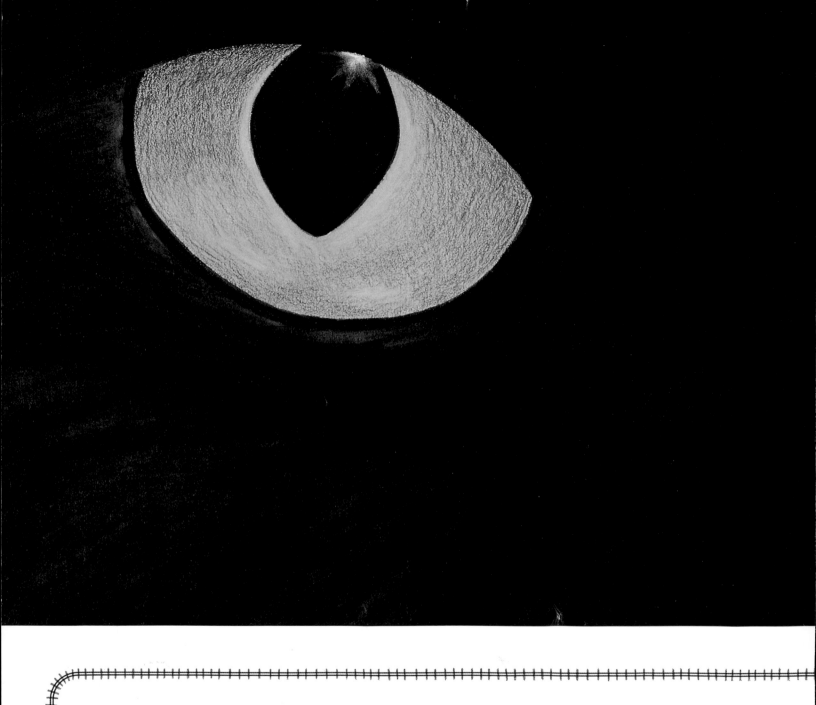

"Oh no, Trouble on the tracks!

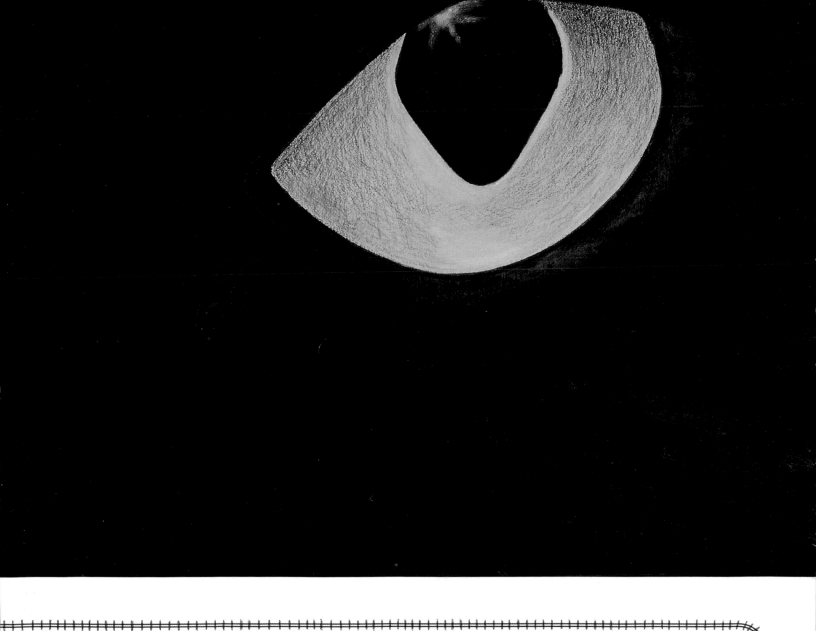

WATCH OUT!" he yells and blasts the whistle.

"Not again!"

He looks over the damage and shakes his head.

This is not the first time the engineer's cat,
Trouble, has lived up to her name.

But it had better be the last.

With the train out of action, Trouble's fun is over for now.

The mischievous cat moves on.

The engineer begins his repairs.

He rights each piece and puts it back on the tracks in its proper order. Then he resets the fallen trees.

With Trouble out of sight, the engineer
sounds the whistle once again. The train
continues on its way.

It rolls through forests and farmland. It rumbles
through villages where faces are familiar . . .

and Trouble sometimes lurks.